CASTING
A SPELL

CASTING A SPELL
AND OTHER POEMS
An Anthology of New Poems

Compiled by
ANGELA HUTH

Illustrations by
JANE RAY

ORCHARD BOOKS

For my daughter Eugenie, her friends Lucinda Leachman
and Polly Wilson, and all other children who share the
same delight in poetry.

Dream Song, Shoes © Joan Aiken 1991; *Mr Simpson and His Cat* © Kingsley Amis 1991; *Cats* © Simon Armitage 1991; *November* © George Barker 1991; *Tumbling Cliff* © Pam Beasant 1991; *The Caged Bird* © Veronica Bennetts 1991; *Mistaken Identity* © Don Black 1991; *The Day that Jack Frost Came, Ice Cream, Chocolate Biscuits and Jam* © Edwin Brock 1991; *The Lion and the Unicorn, Not Fair* © Lucy Coats 1991; *The Baby of the Family* © Wendy Cope 1991; *The Lincoln Imp, The Meeting of the Ways* © June Crebbin 1991; *Choosing* © Quentin Crewe 1991; *The World Inside the World* © Kevin Crossley-Holland 1991; *Badger, Quieter than Snow* © Berlie Doherty 1991; *Rhyming Roland* © Richard Edwards 1991; *In Case You're Wondering* © Max Fatchen 1991; *On the Mountain* © John Fuller 1991; *At the Seaside, Conquering Shyness, Don't Quite Know,* © Roy Fuller 1991; *Is It Fair?* © Nigel Gray 1991; *The Ghost of Gruesome Towers* © John Heath-Stubbs 1991; *An Enquiring Mind* © Douglas Houston 1991; *Crab, Jellyfish* © Ted Hughes 1991; *The Panchen Lama Rides from Lhasa to Kumbum* © Kathleen Jamie 1991; *Casting a Spell, Considering Magic, Spell of the Earth* © Elizabeth Jennings 1991; *Timesong* © P. J. Kavanagh 1991; *Charlie* © Herbert Kretzmer 1991; *Nest, Treasure* © Una Leavy 1991; *Home* © Peter Levi 1991; *Limericks* © Bernard Levin 1991; *Tree* © Brian McCabe 1991; *James, Upside-down Rubber Boot* © Fiona MacInnes 1991; *Our Pier: Orkney* © George Mackay Brown 1991; *Saints* © Candia McWilliam 1991; *In Love?, A Thinking Christmas* © Wes Magee 1991; *I Walk Two Dogs* © Adrian Mitchell 1991; *Seahorse* © Blake Morrison 1991; *Riddle* © Judith Nicholls 1991; *All You Want to Do* © Julie O'Callaghan 1991; *Be Careful with Those Apples — They Don't Grow On Trees, You Know!* © David Profumo 1991; *Boats* © Alan Ross 1991; *Mothers Who Don't Understand* © Augusta Skye 1991; *The Burglar* © Matthew Sweeney 1991; *Jack's Poem* © Anthony Thwaite 1991; *A Warning to Cat Owners* © Sue Townsend 1991; *Dark Thoughts* © Fred Warner 1991; *Comet, Think of It* © Zaro Weil 1991; *Holy Snails* © John Wells 1991; *An Angry Alligator* © Colin West 1991; *Boring* © John Whitworth 1991; *Pity Your Parents* © Roger Woddis 1991.

ORCHARD BOOKS
96 Leonard Street
London EC2A 4RH
Orchard Books Australia
14 Mars Road, Lane Cove, NSW 2066

First published in Great Britain in 1991
This selection copyright © Angela Huth 1991
Decorations copyright © Jane Ray 1991

The right of Angela Huth to be identified as the compiler of this
work, and of Jane Ray as the illustrator, has been asserted by
them in accordance with the Copyright, Designs and Patents Act, 1988.

A CIP catalogue record for this book is available from the British Library.

1 85213 290 6

Printed in Singapore

Contents

Seahorse

O under the ocean waves
I gallop the seaweed lanes,
I jump the coral reef,
And all with no saddle or reins.

I haven't a flowing mane,
I've only this horsey face,
But under the ocean waves
I'm king of the steeplechase.

Blake Morrison

The Baby of the Family

Up on Daddy's shoulders
He is riding high –
The baby of the family,
A pleased, pork pie.
I'm tired and my feet are sore –
It seems all wrong.
He's lucky to be little
But it won't last long.

The baby of the family,
He grabs my toys
And when I grab them back he makes
A big, loud noise.
I mustn't hit him, so I chant
This short, sweet song:
"You're lucky to be little
But it won't last long."

Everybody looks at him
And thinks he's sweet,
Even when he bellows "No!"
And stamps his feet.
He won't be so amusing
When he's tall and strong.
It's lovely being little
But it won't last long.

Wendy Cope

A Warning to Cat Owners

Cats don't have a Highway Code,
They like the freedom of the road.
Our cat, called Zoe, soft and nice,
Ignored the signs and paid the price.
She tried to beat the rush hour traffic,
We fetched a shoe box from the attic.
We dug a grave behind the shed,
And there we laid poor Zoe's head.
We sang a song and gathered flowers,
We cried until the early hours.
But cats don't have a Highway Code,
They like the freedom of the road.

Sue Townsend

Not Fair

He stole the matches.
Nicked them off Mum's tray,
Last Tuesday morning, early,
When he came round to play.

I built a house.
A window and a door.
The open sky my ceiling
And wildweed for my floor.

He built a fire
In our old hollow tree.
Fuelled its hungry flames with grass.
I didn't see.

Evening wisps of subtle smoke,
Fire's tearing fangs.
Big red engines. Bells ringing.
CLANG! CLANG! CLANG!

Scolded. Banished. Punished. Weeping.
Turn the bedroom key.
Angry Mum. Crosser Dad.
Why did they blame *me*?

Lucy Coats

The Lion and the
Unicorn

The lion and the unicorn were eating bread and cheese
When suddenly a crumptious smell came wafting on the breeze.
"It's plum cake," snorted Unicorn, "all moist and warm and
    brown!"
"It's lemon pie, with ginger crust!" growled Lion, with a frown.
"It is!", "It's not!", "It's not!", "It is!". Around and round they
    went,
Until each one was not quite sure just what the other meant.
The lion pawed and pounced and lashed, and danced about
    the street.
The unicorn with horn and hoof struck sparks round people's
    feet.

And, "One to Lion!", cried the crowd. And, "Unicorn,
    Halloo!".
And pushed and shoved and punched and kicked to get a
    better view.
Up and down and through the town, right to the castle door
The battle raged and ramped and roared as fiercely as before.
Till Ulf the King in robes of green, and crown of gold and
    red
Said, "Stop! How dare you wake me from my comfy Royal
    bed?
"I cannot sleep, I cannot eat, I cannot rule the land!
"I cannot even *hear* the music from my Royal Band!"
Ashamed, the lion hung his mane and crept away to hide.
But Unicorn just stamped a hoof and ground his teeth with
    pride.
Next day the trumpeters proclaimed by Royalest Decree,
"The King has banished Unicorn beyond his boundary.
"If he comes back, or speaks a word, or even dares to sneeze,
"Then Lion can go and crunch him up for breakfast (plus his
    fleas)!"
The lion licked the Royal hand as meekly as a mouse.
The King made him the mascot of the ruling Royal House.
But Unicorn crept out of town at dawn without a sound.
And that is why you never see a unicorn around.

Lucy Coats

Treasure

Judith goes to feed the hens
plaits down her back
legs bare in navy shorts
– the bucket's red.
Lifting the latch
of the wire mesh gate
she steps in the hen-run,
Rhode Island reds
rush in a tumbled fuss
of featherness
hustling for grain.

Six nesting-boxes
huddle in the shade
sheltered from sun
six eggs are laid
smudgy with mud
fuzzy with hen-down.

Carefully now
into the bucket
    one
        by
            one
dying to tell
longing to yell
but she mustn't run.
Tenderly now
past rhubarb and sage
by lupins and hollyhocks
"Nanna!" she calls,
"I've got them all
— an egg for every box!"

Una Leavy

Nest

Once on a dappled Winter's night we went
wrapped in our scarves
over the frost-stiff grass.
The night was still
except for our crackling feet
and the creak
of Tom's arthritic knee.
He stopped when we reached the trees
then lifting the candle lantern
over our heads
showed us the nest —
brown speckled feathers
slit eyes
small silent beaks
hearts beating
breath breathing
wild things in their resting
stirring their fragile wings . . .

We did not speak.

Turning for home
we quenched the candle flame;
in the distance a dog barked,
somebody coughed,
nothing was the same.

Una Leavy

Casting a Spell

Learn a spell. It takes some time
First you must have the gift of rhyme,
New images, a melody.
Verse will do but poetry
Sometimes will come if you have luck.
Play tunes, blow trumpets, learn to pluck
The harp. The best of spells are cast
When you have written words to last,
Rich in subtle rhythms and
Right words which most will understand.
Casting a spell's a secret skill
Which few learn fast. No act of will
On your part hands the gift to you.
Words must surprise and yet ring true.
False sorcerers are everywhere
But the true magic's deep and rare.

Elizabeth Jennings

Spell of the Earth

I am the round of the globe,
The seas are my green robe,
I am where all plants grow
   And the trees know

From me they draw their strength,
From me all stems find length.
I am rich in countless ways,
   All footsteps give me praise.

Elizabeth Jennings

Tumbling Cliff

The cliff falls head-first
into the sea. It lies asleep,
not dead, for sea-weed
sprouts on its head, and the sea
combs it with the care of a child.

Pam Beasant

Upside-down Rubber Boot

Upside-down rubber boot with a tail
That's what you remind me of today
Shiny black selkie
Slipping in and out
Of the silvery blue sea.

Fiona MacInnes

*'Selkie' is the Orcadian word for a seal. The poet lives
on the island of Orkney in Scotland.*

James

"No friends for James
No friends for James to play with"
Trailed the solo voice
From the children's chorus
Small size malice
Coming home from school

And as I passed
There scuffed the friendless target
James who made me smile inside
But then feel sad
To see his public hurt

We saw him cry
The new boy
That no one liked
Smug persecutors we
With our collective right

"No friends for James to play with
No friends for James
Oh what a shame
No friends for James"

And walking on I saw
His open tears
And felt his small boy hurt
And nearly turned around
To set the record straight.

Fiona MacInnes

I Walk Two Dogs

(for Ella and Judy)

I walk two dogs.
On her black lead and chain
Trots my Marilyn Monroe retriever
With all her golden feathers flowing.

I walk two dogs.
On her small red lead
Runs an old Jack Russell like a country aunt.
Just above her tail she wears a large black blot
Which indicates where she likes to be patted.

I walk two dogs,
Their paths are intertwined.
When we reach Hampstead Heath and their freedom
They glance around, making up their minds
Where we're supposed to go.

Monroe's an archaeologist,
Her aunt is an explorer.
So the retriever digs with paws and nose
While the Jack Russell gets as lost as she can.
I go for walks in two directions at once,
Though sometimes they graze on the scents in the grass,
Muzzles together in the smoky early morning.

I call them to me, I fix their leads.
As I follow them home I feel like the sail
Of a ship of gold and black and white.
I walk two dogs,
I walk two dogs,
I walk them on two leads
Held in one hand.

Footnote to "I Walk Two Dogs"

I boastfully wrote I Walk Two Dogs,
Then went to catch a bus and met a fellow
Walking six greyhounds on their leads
Dressed in long coats of black and yellow.
They were strong and perfectly-formed and clean,
Like the components of a submarine.

Adrian Mitchell

Cats

Are safe, and stealing sleep in quiet curls
around the house, keeping secrets to themselves,
easily. Their lips are sealed, their tails are question marks
or ride up behind them like dodgem car hooks.

We love cats. They shred the settee and we sit there
and let them, we buy them toys or collars with bells on,
we give them our names and the warmest places
and behind our backs they are licking their faces.

The last cat to cross my path was a white one,
at night. Fast and silent like a shooting star
till it stopped, looked me up and down and blinked
then walked away, as if I was no one, leaving me cold

as if I'd been caught, or photographed, or shot at,
or had my wallet stolen. Cats are something else,
worlds away, and we are welcome to it,
this lump of rock in space we call our planet.

Simon Armitage

Boats

Often we remember their names,
Seagull, Lucy, Victoria, Treasure,
When those of old friends escape us.
Boats remind us of pleasure.

Rowed erratically in estuaries or bays,
Sailed round lochs or up rivers,
They belong to happy-seeming days
Of salt water and canvas.

When summer is over, everyone gone,
The boats — names and paint
Faded — board up their magic,
Tar smell, like scent, lingering on.

Alan Ross

The Burglar

When the burglar went out
to burgle a house

When the burglar pulled on
his black polo-neck,
his beret, his Reeboks

When the burglar rattled
his skeleton keys,
checked he had his street-map,
said goodbye to his budgie

When the burglar shouldered
an empty bag, big enough
to take as much swag
as the burglar could carry

When the burglar waited
for the bus

When the burglar stood
at the bottom of the street
where the house he'd picked
to burgle was

When the burglar burgled
he didn't know
that another burglar
was inside *his* house

And only the budgie would see

Matthew Sweeney

In Case You're Wondering . . .

I want for Christmas . . .
. . . Let me see . . .
I want your spending
Time with me.

I want your jokes
Around my place,
And how you pull
A funny face.

I want your laughter
And your chat.
I want your smile
I DO want that.

I want your eyes
Of dancing blue.
I want a nice
Fat present too.

Max Fatchen

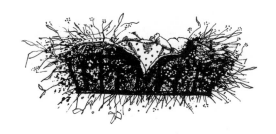

A Thinking Christmas

A turkey dinner
at Christmas is great!

THINK

Somewhere . . . a boy
with an empty plate.

The Christmas tree lights
shine red, green and gold.

THINK

Somewhere . . . a girl
shivering and cold.

Presents and parties!
Yes, *that's* Christmas Day!

THINK

Somewhere . . . a babe
asleep in the hay.

Wes Magee

In love?

Our Miss Gill
and Mr Scott
seem to like
each other
rather a lot.
His class
and our class
are always going
on trips together.
Today we climbed
Tucker's Hill
in *dreadful* weather.
"He held her hand."
"Never!"
"He did, and they kissed."
"No!"
It turned terribly cold.
"I'm freezing," said Jill.
It started to rain,
then there was sleet,
and then snow.

At least
it was warm
on the coach,
and we all sang.
Arrived at the school gate
just as the bell rang.
Off we trooped home.
At the street corner
I turned
and looked back.
So did Jill.
We watched
and our Miss Gill
crossed the car park
hand in glove
with Mr Scott.
"They are in love,"
said Jill.
Yes, they do seem
to like each other
rather a lot.

Wes Magee

The Panchen Lama Rides
from Lhasa to Kumbum

(A thousand miles in a single night)

Now the sky is saddled with stars,
a saddle of stars thrown over the hills' back;
night is a horse leaping the mountains,
night is a nomad shifted by morning,
the Panchen Lama rides hard out of Lhasa
low and clung to the horse's mane,
clings to the mane strung like a comet,
and clear of the darkened backstreets, chants
to the ready ear, pale as a conch shell
the thousandth tantra's thousandth cycle,
and horse and Lama quit their earthly forms.

That night a wind crossed snow and pasture;
ruffled the feathers of sleeping rivers,
whirled like a cloak round the shoulders of mountains.
The plateau of Tibet
stretched away like an oil-dark painting
to the grassland, where in tethered yurts
families wrapped in yaks-wool, slept;
and warm-flanked yaks shifted in their dreaming,
and certain dogs
who opened their jaws to the flying hoof-beat,
with an invisible gesture of the Lama's hand
were silenced and charmed.

So for a thousand miles;
till the sun coaxed the world to open like a daisy;
splashed gold on the roofs of the gold-roofed monastery,
on the far side of the precious and protecting hill
at will assumed their mortal shape,
slowed to a canter and entered by the courtyard,
and the youngest boy-monk who rushed from the temple,
his face round as a gong of wonder
to touch the robes grab the reins receive a blessing,
and though that boy lived to be a hundred
he always swore
the Panchen Lama
winked.

Kathleen Jamie

*The poet discovered this legend at a Tibetan monastery in Kumbum and saw the
horse, now stuffed and very odd. It is believed to be a divine horse, which made this
fantastic journey with the Lama on its back.*

All You Want To Do

Someday you will tell your mother,
    "So sorry – I don't want to visit
    the children's art exhibit".
To your father you will explain,
    "If you don't mind, I'll give that
    young person's concert a miss".
When the doorbell rings, say,
    "Thanks anyway, but I'm not in the mood
    for pancakes and kite-flying".
Supposing your friend invites you, reply,
    "There's no ice-skating and doughnuts
    for me today – maybe I can go next week".
If it's your cousin on the phone, try,
    "Have fun at the movies,
    don't throw popcorn at the screen".

        All you want to do
        is sit in the kitchen
        twirling spaghetti
        onto a fork
        and after that
        stop at the window
        as if watching for snow.

Julie O'Callaghan

Comet

The night crackles with silence
As you fly
Headlong among the stars
Against dark granite
You are a spray of hot gold
Fiery plume of an ancient creature
Frivolous stroke of a molten pen
Breathless orange curve
You cut through boundless sky
A firey race to the future
A dazzle of a second
A moment of the past

Zaro Weil

Think of It

Think of it

The first shudder of damp
That somehow signalled
All was ready

Then
In the deep inside of earth
In the muted underneath of winter
Spring began

Not with a sudden trumpet of green
Or a sky of confetti blossoms
But with a seed
Small, pale and barely breathing

It lay quietly
Waiting for the lavender clouds
That carry the first warm rains

Then
For some reason as ancient and
Everyday as the sun itself

The seed cracked
Split and softly burst into
A faint tendril
A root a sprout
A thin wisp of a growing thing

And
With no thought of stopping
It pushed through the
Dark soil with the force of
A billion winter winds
Until it

Pierced the crust of the outside and
Split the frozen armour of earth

Which has held spring safe
Since time began

Zaro Weil

Choosing

When you start to write a poem, you always have to make a
    choice,
Shall it have a rattling rhythm, or will it use a calmer voice?
I say this merely for example, as it happens all the time,
Life is made up of decisions, not just when you make a
    rhyme.

When you get up in the morning, will you put on red or
    blue?
Tea or coffee, toast or porridge, what exactly will suit you?
And at lunchtime, raspberry pudding? Or would you rather
    have some cheese?
Then again, it sadly may be, you want neither one of these.

Of course, it doesn't really matter, it may even be amusing,
To make a whopping great performance out of all this trivial
    choosing.
The day will come, I have to tell you, when it doesn't seem
    so jolly—
Are you going to marry Milly, or would you rather wed with
    Molly?

I'm sure you want to be a doctor or a soldier or a wife,
Every day your fancy changes, but now the choice is for your
    life.
But think of how you always dither, no wind of sureness fills
    your sails;
It's simple, really, toss a coin and see if you have a heads or
    tails.

Quentin Crewe

Timesong

I went for a wander, I needed a wonder,
Watched the sun rising, and sun gave me one.
It picked out lost places, the angle it shone
At, on hillsides where once stood the houses of men,
Small settlements, traces, by shadows were shown.
If light never changed we would never be gone.

It lit the far farm where we first were together —
You would know and not know it, that new house was its
   barn.
(From places so power-filled I should be gone
Now, as you are. The music you taught me goes on,
Though I know to my bone there's a change in the tune.)
If songs stayed the same they would never be done.

Then, brighter than nature, as though a curator
Of flints made a present, leaf-shaped, a white stone
So knapped and so shaped you could picture the man
Bent over it, chipping, sun picked from the brown.
Between finger and thumb it sat snug to each bone
As I held it and turned it and cried to the sun
Which was high now, the house-ghosts all melted in green,
If you stayed where you were we would never be gone.

P. J. Kavanagh

The Ghost of Gruesome Towers

I am the ghost of Gruesome Towers —
I haunt there, in nocturnal hours,
And do it rather well, because
This talent is, and always was
A kind of speciality
In our distinguished family.

My grandad was a hideous Ghoul
Who came, I'm told, from Istanbul,
His wife, the Lady Hypermania,
A vampiress from Transylvania.
Her story has a tragic twist —
An interfering exorcist
Destroyed in — I have to say —
A most ungentlemanly way.
He staked her through the heart — to boot,
He stuffed her full of garlic-root.

My auntie is a Bleeding Nun —
I'm told she gets a lot of fun
Through haunting a monastic grange.
She has a quite surprising range
Of gibberings, and sepulchral groans,
Weird wailings, and despairing moans.

My uncle Poltergeist, whose haunt
Is a posh West End restaurant,
Has lately gained a lot of clout
Through throwing pots and pans about –
Sieves, cullenders and nutmeg-graters.
The affluent diners and the waiters
See knives and forks and tableware
Go madly hurtling through the air –
He once hurled a whole dinner service
At Lady Aspidistra Purvis.

My nephew – who's a bright young spark,
And just about to make his mark
(For to go far he has been tipped)
Haunts a damp, gloomy, Gothic crypt.
He's slowly mastering the technique
Of the high-pitched bloodcurdling shriek.
He's just a Nameless Something now,
But soon he'll learn his trade – and how!

I know what you're about to say –
This haunting lark has had its day.
It's all a lot of foolish flummery,
Pretentious and outmoded mummery.
You think I'll never frighten you:
Well just you listen – "Hoo! Hoo!! Hoo!!!"

John Heath-Stubbs

Shoes

Oh my left shoe was sober
But my right shoe was witty
Left wanted a country walk
Right made for the city

Left went trudging into the fields
Right danced up the Mall
What was *I* supposed to do?
I didn't know at all —

That's why, when you see me,
I never speak nor laugh
Always looking for the rest of me:
My shoes pulled me in half

Joan Aiken

Dream Song

listen to my mirror
watch by my bed
listen to my dream
the dark voice said

listen to the sunset
beyond the plain
for I'll not be coming
by this way again
I'll not be able
to tell you again

listen to the oldest road in town
listen to its whisper as the sun goes down
the voice of the rainbow, the voice of bone
the voice of places where people have been

listen to my mirror
mark its gleam
watch by my bed
listen to my dream

the whispers are fading
the sky is dumb
the mirror's faces
are blanched and gone

listen to the sunset
far across the plain
for I'll not be coming
along this way again
I'll not be able
to tell you again

Joan Aiken

Our Pier: Orkney

Mrs Jemima Rendall lives in
    the house with the green door.
She keeps twelve hens in her yard
And a fierce red cockerel that
    would leap at you like a flame.

Bella Swann lives in the house with
    the broken window.
She takes in grubby washing
And carries out snow-white layers
    in her basket to the
    lawyers' wives and the
    shopkeepers' wives and the
    minister's wife.

Mrs Roberta Wylie sings all day in
    the house above the sea.
She has six cats
Who all go insane when Tom Wylie
    comes back from the west
    with his boat *Daystar* full
    of fish.

My mother lives in the house next
      the street.
She brightens my face with water
      every morning.
"Now", she says, "do what the teacher tells you,
      and you learned your seven times table last
      night — and no fighting with other
      boys, especially Jackie Spence that bully" —
      then she kisses me and gives me a penny.

Miss Audrey Thomson lives in the
      house with lace curtains
And she speaks very proper.
She worked in a lawyer's office in
      Edinburgh for years, now she gives
      piano lessons to the stupid sons
      and daughters of sea captains.

Old Annie Grimsness, she lives in a
      stone hut
But her cabbages and tatties
Are bigger than everyone else's,
      also she can tell what the
      weather will be the day after
      tomorrow, judging by the phase of
      the moon and the piece of dry
      seaweed she keeps on her wall,
      and she's better than any wireless
      weatherman.

George Mackay Brown

The Caged Bird

You can catch me, you can bind me,
You can tether me and tie me,
You can lock me in a cage of gold
And fasten tight my wings;
You can treat me as your property,
Release me three times daily,
But you cannot trap my spirit
And you cannot steal my song.

Veronica Bennetts

Is It Fair?

Is is fair to keep a fish in a bowl?
Is it fair to keep a bird in a cage?
If *you* were kept in a prison
would you fly in a terrible rage?
Imagine that you are a monkey,
an ape, or a chimpanzee.
Would you like to be kept in a zoo?
Or do you think you might rather be free?

Nigel Gray

Boring

I'm dead bored,
  bored to the bone.
Nobody likes me,
  I'm all alone.
I'll just go crawl
  under a stone.

Hate my family,
  got no friends,
I'll sit here till
  the universe ends
Or I starve to death –
  it all depends.

Then I'll be dead,
  dead and rotten,
Less than a blot when
  it's been well blotten,
Less than a teddy bear
  that's been forgotten.

Then I'll go to Heaven which
    is more than can be said
For certain persons
    when they're dead.
They'll go you-know-
    where instead.

Then they'll be sorry,
    Then they'll be glum,
Sitting on a stove till
    Kingdom Come.
Then they can all go
    kiss my . . .

Hmm, that's a sort of swearing;
    people shouldn't swear.
I won't go to Heaven but
    I don't care,
    I don't care,
    I don't care.
I'll sit here and swear
    so there.

Except that it's boring . . .
                John Whitworth

An Enquiring Mind

– for Iggy

Dad, who invented numbers
And how did they agree
The order they should go in,
How many there should be?

Why is it lead's so heavy
While balsa wood's so light?
If ghosts aren't real, why was I scared
Of ghosts the other night?

You told me how the moon pulls tides,
Why stars fade when night's done
(Seems obvious now: they go quite pale
Competing with the sun);

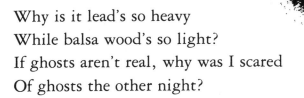

I asked you what the clouds were
So now I think I know
That sky-fluff's water-vapour
Borne where the winds will blow;

You said that stuff called chlorophyll
Makes leaves and grasses green –
But why are roses mainly red
And a blue one's never seen?

Why is it mountains are so big
And why do roofs have tiles?
Is it further to America
In kilometres or miles?

For some time I've been wondering
How apple cores go brown,
And why are colours what they are?
Can water-snakes still drown?

Thanks for the encyclopaedia, Dad.
The dictionary's good, too;
But when it comes to finding out
It's quicker asking you.

Douglas Houston

The Meeting of
the Ways

The Motorway said, "I'm the best by far,
I am built for the high-speed car."

The High Street said, "No, I'm the tops,
In me you'll find all the well-known shops."

"Trees line me," said the Avenue,
"I'm the obvious choice of the well-to-do."

Said the quiet Close, "They choose me too.
I'm sure I'm nearly as good as you."

The Crescent cried, "I go right round the bend.
You'll never find me with a blocked-off end!"

The Cul-de-sac at once replied,
"But I am calm and dignified."

"Which way is best is hard to agree,"
Said the mighty Drive. "But I'm sure it's me."

Under the blue and cloudless sky
The footpath quietly passed them by.
He made his way to the top of the hill:
And across the fields he is travelling still.

June Crebbin

The Lincoln Imp

Where skies are black and forests grey,
The Devil sent his Imps to play.
They climbed the wind, they rode the rain,
They danced upon the Devil's brain.
They kicked him and they pulled his horns,
They tickled him with wicked thorns,
Till, furious, the Devil cried,
"I will not have my peace denied.
Hurl them far and hurl them high,
Hang them in the empty sky
And when they thus have spent their days
There to think and mend their ways
Then bring my servants back to me."

The East Wind roared maliciously.
He caught the Imps and leapt on high
To nail them to the angry sky,
And all but two, he fastened there,
Who screamed and fought the rushing air,
These two he chased to Lincoln town,
He tossed them up, he threw them down
But caught them not. They landed, spent,
Within the city's battlement.

Above them rose the Minster's spire,
A pinnacle, as though on fire,
And every jewelled window shone
As brightly as the morning sun.
The Imps could scarce believe their eyes
To see such wonder in the skies.
Up they flew in awe, and yet
One danced upon the parapet
And, to the other, loudly cried,
"I'm not afraid to go inside."

Beneath the Bishop's feet he flew
And tripped him up and then he blew
The candles out and spilt the wine,
And knocked the choirboys out of line.
He perched upon the verger's nose,
He scrambled up and down the rows
Of kneeling congregation. When
He broke the high East Window, then
The Angels spoke and warned him once
To stop his wilful, cruel dance.
The Imp replied, "I've just begun.
You try and stop me. If you can."

And where the Imp had lightly flown
The Angels turned him into stone.
Cross-legged, grotesque, he stares in awe,
Condemned to sit for evermore.

June Crebbin

The Lincoln Imp, whose ancient legend inspired this poem,
is a strange, half-human, half-animal figure, carved
in stone. It may be seen high up between two arches
in the Angel Choir of Lincoln Cathedral.

Rhyming Roland

Round the round world Roland went,
Rhyming place and instrument,

So, on tour in Mexico,
Roland played the piccolo,

Then drove down to hot Caracas
Where he rattled hot maraccas,

Flew to tropical Rangoon,
Serenaded on bassoon,

Travelled northwards to Tibet,
Blew some blues on clarinet,

Moved to Europe, liked Turin,
Stayed and bowed his violin,

Headed west to grey Cologne,
Busked the squares on saxophone,

France was next and chic Bordeaux
Echoed to his twanged banjo,

Crossed the seas to Panama,
Played jazz on a cool guitar,

Then one day in sunny Cuba
As he oompahed on the tuba,

Suddenly he lost his puff.
"Right," said Roland. "That's enough

"All this rhyming stuff must stop!"
Sold his tuba to a shop,

Caught a jumbo jet to Venice,
Took up tennis.

Richard Edwards

Jellyfish

When my chandelier
Waltzes pulsing near
Let the swimmer fear.

Beached and bare
I'm less of a scare.
But I don't care.

Though I look like a slob
It's a delicate job
Being just a blob.

Ted Hughes

Crab

In the low tide pools
I pack myself like
A handy pocket
Chest of tools.

But as the tide fills
Dancing I go
Under lifted veils
Tiptoe, tiptoe.

And with pliers and pincers
Repair and remake
The daintier dancers
The breakers break.

Ted Hughes

Mr Simpson and His Cat

Old Mr Simpson lived alone
But not precisely on his own.
The best way to make sense of that
Is to explain he kept a cat.
That is, he kept her warm and fed,
But she kept him, it should be said,
From—well, from going off his head
With loneliness and lovelessness.
She was quite plain, I must confess,
Black as the ace of spades, without
A fleck of white from tail to snout,
No pretty ways, no clever tricks,
Called Floss. But wait. Each night at six,
When Mr Simpson took his tot
Of gin, he'd offer her a shot:
"Come on, old Flossie, try a sip,
Simply for the companionship."

But no, she wouldn't turn a hair,
She'd just pretend he wasn't there;
Most disappointing. Ah, but then
There came a gloomy evening when
The north wind had begun to blow,
The streets were dark and deep in snow,
And, almost wishing he were dead,
Old Simpson poured his gin and said,
"Well, Flossie, would you like a shot?"
And clearly heard her say, "Why not?"
So then they settled down to chat
Of kittens, neighbours, dogs, all that,
Of all the years they'd spent together
And faced their share of stormy weather,
How Floss was once stuck in a tree,
And Mr Simpson got her free,
The time he fell and hit his head,
And Floss yowled fit to wake the dead
Until the upstairs tenant's wife
Heard her—which saved the old boy's life.
The time went by. I rather think
They must have had another drink
And Mr Simpson thereupon
Put some of his old records on,
And said to Flossie, "Shall we dance?"
And with fantastic elegance
The pair of them moved to and fro
(With slow and slow and quick-quick slow)
Across that little sitting-room
To 'Sweetie Pie' and 'Love in Bloom'.

The hour of midnight came at last,
The time of wonderland was past;
Old Simpson sank into his chair,
And some hours later woke up there
Feeling distinctly worse for wear.
What he remembered of last night
Seemed crazy in the morning light:
A dream, he thought—he knew it was
As soon as Flossie showed, because
When he called out, "Hallo, my dear,"
She hardly found it worth a sneer;
She didn't even turn a hair,
Pretended he just wasn't there.
Well, so it goes, he thought, that's that;
Of course, she's no more than a cat.

That morning, following routine,
Mrs Malone came in to clean,
And, as she always did, picked up
Old Mr Simpson's coffee-cup,
His empty glass—but half a minute,
There was a second glass, and in it
A dozen strands of jet-black hair.
Mrs Malone said, "I declare!
That's something to be wondered at!
No one comes here; there's just the cat."

Kingsley Amis

November

The saddest month is November,
    But noble as an old
Magician who can turn the mist
    Into mysterious gold.

This dark and cloudy king presides
    Over the dying sun,
That sun which, as it departs,
    Draws winter's chariot on.

George Barker

Mistaken Identity

I'd make a terrible witness.

If I saw a bank raid
I wouldn't know if they wore stocking masks,
if they were short, tall, black or green.

I'm just no good at those things.

I still can't tell a gladioli from a rhododendron
or a robin from a starling
and if I'm honest I never noticed Gorbachev's birthmark
till it was pointed out to me.

But when I think of you
I see so clearly the shape of your
eager hands as you attack your vanilla ice cream with the
coconut topping

That dopey expression as you realise you forgot to tape
Top Of The Pops

The laughter in your eyes when I show you my Donald Duck
impression

The way your freckles seem to catch fire when the tyres on
your bike go flat

The way your body wobbles when you skip

If I ever see you rob a bank
your number's up.

Don Black

Jack's Poem

for my grandson, Jack Sanderson Thwaite

There is a man who cannot stand fat meat,
Who (with his Jill) went uphill on his feet,
Who joins a Union that makes a flag,
Who lives inside a box and not a bag,
Who is a jolly sailor (and a rabbit),
Who climbs a beanstalk, and who makes a habit
Of eating plums in puddings. You could play
A sort of dressed-up chimneysweep in May,
Or games with him — when turned into five stones.
Or he becomes an animal that groans
Eee-aw Eee-aw, and then into a bird
Much like a thieving crow. His name's a word
That goes with lanterns, offices, pots, boots,
Lifts cars, makes frost, can cut, diverts planes' routes.
He killed a frightful Giant. Though not a master
Of trades at all, his diving is much faster
Than any bellyflop. In politics
He was called Straw, a man of knavish tricks.
Robinson's one name — but, tell me, can you say
Something before it which gives my game away?

Anthony Thwaite

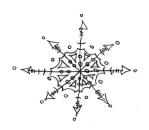

The Day that Jack Frost Came

Sally said, Let's build a sledge
The day that Jack Frost came
Let's build a snowman by the hedge
The day that Jack Frost came
So Sally and
The other two
Piled up snow
Till their hands
Were blue
And their toes
And noses too
The day that Jack Frost came

Klosky said, Snow's better than rain
The day that Jack Frost came
Better for stars on the window pane
The day that Jack Frost came
Better for seeing
The way your words
Fly from your lips
Like big white birds
And disappear
In misty curls
The day that Jack Frost came

Hannah said, Singing's the thing to do
The day that Jack Frost came
The Christmas songs we know right through
The day that Jack Frost came
So they sang about
Robins and mistletoe
When all the world
Was white with snow
And donkeys in places
Long ago
The day that Jack Frost came

They ran in the snow with their tongues stuck out
The day that Jack Frost came
To taste it cold and wet in their mouths
The day that Jack Frost came
And when the day
Was turning red
They hadn't had time
To build a sled
So said tomorrow
Would do instead
The day that Jack Frost came

They called goodnight and went three ways
The day that Jack Frost came
And said, Today of all their days
The day that Jack Frost came
Had been as good
As birthday cakes
And favourite dolls
And roller skates
And all the games
A snowstorm makes
The day that Jack Frost came.

Edwin Brock

Ice cream and Chocolate Biscuits and Jam

I don't like bread
and I don't like butter
and I won't be fed
on bacon for my supper

    for ice cream and chocolate
    biscuits and jam
    made me the kind of a girl
    that I am.

I don't like cheese
(you can keep it for the mice)
and I don't think peas
are particularly nice

    but ice cream and chocolate
    biscuits and jam
    made me the kind of a girl
    that I am.

I don't like fish
(you can leave it in the sea)
I don't like spinach
and it doesn't like me

    it was ice cream and chocolate
    biscuits and jam
    made me the kind of a girl
    that I am.

My parents say
I will get fatter and fatter
if I have my way
but it doesn't much matter

    give me ice cream and chocolate
    biscuits and jam
    for they made me the kind of a girl
    that I am.

Edwin Brock

Pity Your Parents

My Gran once said, "Remember, lad,
You must be kind to Mum and Dad:
They do the best they can, poor things;
Angels they aren't, they don't have wings."

It must be quite a strain to be
Responsible for kids like me.
I'm sure it drives them up the wall,
Pretending that they know it all.

"Your room's a mess" – "Don't tease the cat" –
"I've warned you – don't use words like that!"
They're never wrong, they're always right.

No wonder they can't sleep at night.

Roger Woddis

Limericks

There was a young man who said, "Run!
  The end of the world has begun.
  A green thing with a spoon
  Has just eaten the moon,
  And is now getting down to the sun."

There was a young man who said, "Damn!
  I am covered all over in jam.
  The wasps and the bees
  Are stinging my knees,
  Next time I'll eat nothing but ham."

There was a young fellow called Fred
  Who always ate dinner in bed.
  When his wife asked him not to
  He said, "I have got to,
  Or sleep in the oven instead."

There was an old man in a boat,
  Who was perfectly sure he could float.
  "Just watch me," he cried,
  And jumped over the side:
  But the only thing found was his coat.

Bernard Levin

71

Conquering Shyness

When I was young I was so shy
That if I saw a passer-by
I knew, I made to cross the street
Or gazed into the empty sky
Or at my fascinating feet.

Children, beware of shyness now —
It may last through your adult life.
And I myself must wonder how
I came on stage and took a bow,
And married a most beauteous wife.

Roy Fuller

Don't Quite Know

Why do I feel excited
When chance decides for us
We are to sit together
In an ordinary school bus?
    Don't quite know.

You pick me for your team (or
More likely I'm the one
Left over for your picking) –
Why is that such great fun?
    Don't quite know.

In the game or on the journey
My bare knee touches yours.
If only for a moment
I see strange opening doors.
    Why that is so
    I don't quite know.

Roy Fuller

At the Seaside

Each day the children crumple up the beach.
And twice a day the ocean smoothes it out.

Sand is once-living shells, and rock, ground fine
Through millions of years before the children came.

And in some future time the sea will still
Continue smoothing, though quite needlessly.

Roy Fuller

On the Mountain

Grass scars
Of snow.
Drifts blow.
There's Mars!
Cloud bars
Still show
Though no
Bright stars.
Half-light.
A fox
Stilts by.
Then night
Unlocks
The sky!

John Fuller

Tree

From the depths of my roots
to the tips of my leaves,
I am tree. I am tree. I am tree.
I am evergreen deciduous coniferous
massive Oak and mini Bonsai.
I am Rowan and I am Silver Birch.
Beech – or, if you prefer, *Fagus Sylvatica*.
Call me what you will, Man.
It makes no difference to me.
I am tree. I am tree. I am tree.

Do you like me? Do you like my trunk?
What does it remind you of?
An elephant's foot? A massive rope of wood?
What about my bark? Does it make you think
of a rhino's horn? The scales of fish?
And satin? And silk? What else?
My skins are as various as my names.
What do you make of my branches?
The bare, slender arms of a girl, maybe?
But with an old woman's elbows.
In her gnarled arthritic fingers
she clasps the nests of birds.
How do you feel about my roots?
Do they seem to wriggle, to writhe?
They've been mistaken for snakes.
And what about my fruit?
Is it still forbidden to you?
Who forbade it? I didn't.

I am root. Branch. Leaf. Sap.
Bark. Blossom. Bud. I am tree.
Without me a flat horizon would be
a flat horizon.

When you look at me, Man, you see
fuel, timber, a table, pulp, paper —
would you make a book out of me?
But it would not have leaves like these.

I am older than you, Man.
I was there in your garden of Eden,
and before: my roots go deeper than you know,
deep into your heart and deeper still.
They clasp the bones of your ancestors
and go deeper yet. I mean more to you
than you know, Man. Why else
would you carve your hearts in me?
Your saws and your axes will not fell me.
Don't underestimate me. I'll outlive you.

Come and sit in the cool shade of my bole.
Beneath the thatched roof of my branches.
Lean against my bark, close your eyes.
Breathe deeply. Now, feel what I am.
I am tree. I am tree. I am tree.

Brian McCabe

Saints

St. Ocking is the saint for socks
St. Ar for the deep black night
St. Icking Plaster for after shocks
St. Ew for a tough old bite

St. Ickleback's the man for stings,
St. Alagmite for drips,
St. Amp for postage, sending things,
St. Eak goes well with chips.

Who's your particular favourite one?
St. Egosaur for dunces?
St. Itch for what you get at a run?
St. Ick 'Em Up as the man with the gun says?

St. Ick is the holy man for glue —
Or, on his day off, for hockey —
The naming of the saints is over to you;
St. Ink!
St. Ingy!
St. Ocky!

Candia McWilliam

78

"Charlie"

Mooses come from Moos-issippi
Cats from Katmandu
Rhinos come from the River Rhine
And kittens from Purr-oo
Parrots come from Polly-nesia
(So the story goes)
But where our puppy Charlie comes from
Goodness only knows!

Rabbits come from Bunny Scotland
(Where they breed in hordes)
Beetles come from Liverpool
And crickets come from Lords.
Elephants come from Tuscaloosa
Bucks from Timbuctoo
But where our puppy Charlie comes from
Haven't got a clue!

Honeybears hail from Honey-lulu
(As you may have guessed)
Blubber comes from Wales, of course,
And Robins come from Brest.
Otters come from Ottawa
And Pekes from Picardy
But where our puppy Charlie comes from
Don't
ask
me!

Herbert Kretzmer

Dark Thoughts

A Fox came to our house one night;
   he stood on the lawn and watched.
He lowered his brush and lifted his head to point
   the moon.
Had he come for my father – to teach him a
   little craft?
Or drawn by the stale smell Dad carries
   from the locker-room?

A Badger came to our house one night and
   rattled the dustbin lid.
She chased it up and down the concrete apron
   at the back.
Had she come for my mother, to strew her rubbish
   over the grass?
Or just to feed on her sliced bread, old stew and
   other muck?

Last night a Rat came to our house and crawled
   up the drain-pipe.
He looked through my brother's window, grinned and
   went into the dark.
Did he come to tell Tommy something black, or to teach
   him fright?
Or has he only brought us fleas and bad luck?

Tonight, an Owl has come to our house and sits in the tree.
He came with a shadow that doubled the
   darkness of night.
He has waited so many weeks to come for me.
Now I must cross my arms and hold my heart in my
   breast.

Sir Fred Warner

Be Careful with Those Apples —
They Don't Grow on Trees,
You Know!

When somebody important, like the Mayor
Or an old boy who is a famous footballer,
Comes to school we suddenly get a terrific meal.
They give us: roast potatoes
                   slices of chicken
                   peas with some sort of sauce.

At the beginning, Mr Wetherby stands up
And says Grace, wearing his special tie.
We have ice cream to finish, and fruit.
Fresh fruit from the school orchard.
Most days, we have tinned pears.

My mum cooks pancakes for us at home;
She says they can't do that at school
Because it would be too difficult.
She makes us: apricot pie
                   banana bread
                   cheesey pizza with runny tomato.
The name of our cook is Mrs Mary.
She's fat. We call her the Big Canary.

On Speech Day, she suddenly produces: scones with jam
                                                sandwiches with
                                                      ham
                                                and little cakes with
                                                     cherries on.

But when we get rubber hot dogs
We hide them behind the pipes.
The shepherd's pie with fish-bones
We hide in our handkerchiefs and
Dump in the yard, like prisoners-of-war
getting rid of earth from a secret tunnel.

They give us: semolina with a crust
                    pasta dry as worms in dust
                    beans like beetles baked in rust.

Why does our food have to be
Frozen or dried in some factory?
Our school has fruit fresh on the tree,
But none of it finds its way to me.
When I grow up, I'm going to teach –
And every boy will have a peach:
The fruits of school should not begin
With something dished up from a tin.

David Profumo

The World Inside the World

I liked Edmund Waller.
His ocean smile was gentle
and he blushed around his collar

– maybe he still does. I remember
the party at his house
on the last day of December

when I was eight.
The party wasn't so special:
it didn't go on late

and Karen wasn't there (my first love);
the cake was just a cake;
no conjuror with rabbit or dove.

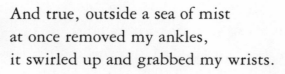

My mother came early to collect me.
"The tide's rising fast," she said,
"it's drowning Aylesbury."

And true, outside a sea of mist
at once removed my ankles,
it swirled up and grabbed my wrists.

Then Edmund's father put one hand
over both my smarting eyes.
"I'll take you back to land,"

he said. "I'll save you from the sea."
First he tripped me sideways,
the half-lifted me

and set me down, nose to flint.
"All right! Open your eyes!"
I peered through a squint

of icy glass into the hollow heart
of his gatepost.
In there, he'd made a world apart –

under a spreading chestnut tree
two laughing boys
(were they Edmund and me?)

were pulling the tail
of an amiable lion,
and a girl with a white pail

was standing by a well
with a thirsty elephant.
A ring of leopards and gazelles

were all admiring her sensible gingham.
Then I knew I'd come
to the Peaceable Kingdom

where nothing moved, nothing died:
this was the world inside the world
without any changing tide

— there were no hopes on fears.
I don't know how long I looked.
I've looked, maybe, for forty years

and each time I turn away
the mist comes lapping round my waist,
silver-white and pearl-grey,

uncertain and beautiful.
Everything is wonderful
and plentiful and dutiful

in the trap of paradise,
but I want change, I want choice:
the unpredictable throw of dice,

the fluctuating human voice,
and sweet and sour, and hot and cold.
Whatever the price,
give me this unfinished world!

Kevin Crossley-Holland

Mothers who Don't Understand

"Why can't you tidy your room?" they cry,
Millions of mothers who fret round the land,
"It's a horrible mess, I've never seen worse,"
– Mothers who don't understand.

They don't understand how cosy it is
To have piles of books on the floor,
And knickers and socks making friends with the vest
Under the bed, where *they* like it best,
And notices pinned to the door.

They don't understand why Kylie and Craig
Are smiling all over the walls,
And toffees and Chewys and dozens of Smarties
Are scattered about reminding of parties,
And jeans are rolled into balls.

They don't understand why a good bed should be
All scrumpled and friendly and gritty,
Why the bears and the paints and the toys are much less
Easy to find if there *isn't* a mess –
To tidy would be a great pity.

They don't understand the point of a desk
Is to balance the muddle quite high:
To leave the drawers open, grow mould on the drink,
Is very much easier, some people think,
Than explaining to mothers just why.

"PLEASE can you tidy your room?" they wail,
Millions of mothers who fret round the land:
"What will you do when there's no one to nag you?"
— Mothers who don't understand.

Augusta Skye

An Angry Alligator

There's no such word as *allegate*,
But what am I to do?
An angry alligator
That I met at London Zoo
Is making allegations
That my theory is untrue.

Colin West

Riddle

I am
pear-drop,
space-hopper
rest-on-a-tail;
fast as a rocket,
and what's in my pocket
small as a snail?
I'm shorter than elephant,
taller than man;
I hop-step-and-jump
as no creature can.
My jacket is fur,
one pocket, not two;
a joey hides there . . .
I am

KANGAROO!

Judith Nicholls

Badger

Through the trees I saw a badger
In the evening, nearly dusk
All the midges dancing round me
Foxglove scent, and ferny musk.

Through the trees I saw a badger
In the twilight, stars just out
Bats like rags were drifting, swooping
Sheep on hillside, farmer's shout

Through the trees I saw a badger
Through the air as grey as smoke
Light as dancers she came listening
Light as ghosts she sniffed the dark

Through the trees I saw a badger
Barred head lifted, wary, keen,
Then she faded through the bracken
Like a whisper, like a dream.

Berlie Doherty

Quieter than Snow

I went to school a day too soon
And couldn't understand
Why silence hung in the yard like sheets
Nothing to flap or spin, no creaks
Or shocks of voices, only air.

And the car park empty of teachers' cars
Only the first September leaves
Dropping like paper. No racks of bikes
No kicking legs, no fights,
No voices, laughter, anything.

Yet the door was open. My feet
Sucked down the corridor. My reflection
Walked with me past the hall.
My classroom smelt of nothing. And the silence
Rolled like thunder in my ears.

At every desk a still child stared at me
Teachers walked through walls and back again
Cupboard doors swung open, and out crept
More silent children, and still more.
They tiptoed round me
Touched me with cold hands
And opened their mouths with laughter that was

Quieter than snow.

Berlie Doherty

Holy Snails

In Paradise the Blessed Snails
They say lay solid silver trails
Advancing with their slow caress
Along the Paths of Righteousness

They have great shells of beaten gold
Bejewelled skirts that spread and fold
Twin pearly horns that search and blink
On stretching necks of diamond link

Gliding beside the Glassy Sea
They weave their shining tracery
Up uncut crags of precious stone
To summits known to God alone

There, high against the emerald sky
They lift their happy horns and sigh
Contented, having laid with Grace
Their winding trail of silver lace

So if you see a snail today
Remember, though its shell is grey
A snail of most especial worth
May lay a silver trail on earth

John Wells

Home

The geese honk, the cock crows, the sheep baa,
You wake in the morning and know where you are.
There are fish in the clay-pit and children in the trees,
And herons make an angry noise that is not meant to please,
The geese are crying overhead trying to keep formation,
And in the middle of the night you hear the railway station.
In the morning farm tractors and then horses go by,
The peacocks merely mope around, they cannot fly so high.
The dogs woof all day long but the cats are quite silent,
Or only snoring in their sleep with purrs of content.
I prefer living where you know where you are,
Where the geese honk, where the cock crows, where the
    sheep baa.

Peter Levi

Considering Magic

Don't think of magic as a conjuring trick
Or just as fortune-tellers reading hands
It is a secret which will sometimes break
Through ordinary days, and it depends

Upon right states of mind like good intent,
A love that's kind, a wisdom that is not
Pleased with itself. This sort of magic's meant
To cast a brilliance on dark trains of thought

And guide you through the mazes of the lost,
Lost love, lost people and lost animals.
For this, a sure, deep spell of care is cast

Which never lies and will not play you false.
It banishes the troubles of the past
And is the oldest way of casting spells.

Elizabeth Jennings

Index of Poems and Poets